A Note to Grown-ups

This book is a book to play with. Feel free to sing, chant or dance the words of the book with the child you are sharing it with. If you can think of new rhymes, new ways to play with the words, do it! The most important thing is that you have fun with words. By playing with words and phrases, we show children that they can explore many different ways to express themselves. I believe that doing this in a fun way helps children to enjoy language and feel free to say what they think and feel. I hope that this book helps your child feel free to talk and use their imagination.

For Joni, love from Zeyde Mick. M.R.

For Elliot. R.S.

First published 2023 by Walker Books Ltd, 87 Vauxhall Walk, London SE11 5HJ

2 4 6 8 10 9 7 5 3 1

Text © 2023 Michael Rosen • Illustrations © 2023 Robert Starling

The right of Michael Rosen and Robert Starling to be identified as author and illustrator respectively of this work has been asserted in accordance with the Copyright, Designs and Patents Act 1988

This work has been typeset in Futura

Printed in China

British Library Cataloguing in Publication Data: a catalogue record for this book is available from the British Library

ISBN 978-1-5295-0658-7

www.walker.co.uk

I AM WRIGGLY

Michael Rosen

ILLUSTRATED BY
Robert Starling

WALKER BOOKS
AND SUBSIDIARIES
LONDON • BOSTON • SYDNEY • AUCKLAND

I am wriggly.

REALLY wriggly.

Wriggly,
wriggly,
wriggly.

I'm SO wriggly ...

my whiskers wiggle,

my ears jiggle,

I wriggle on my chair,

I wriggle with
my bear,

I wriggle round and round,

I wriggle on the ground.

I'm jiggling my spoons,

I'm joggling balloons,

I
juggle
my
socks,

I wiggle in a box.

My boat is bobbling,

my wheels are wobbling,

my kite is squiggly,

my toys higgledy-piggledy.

I wave
my feet,

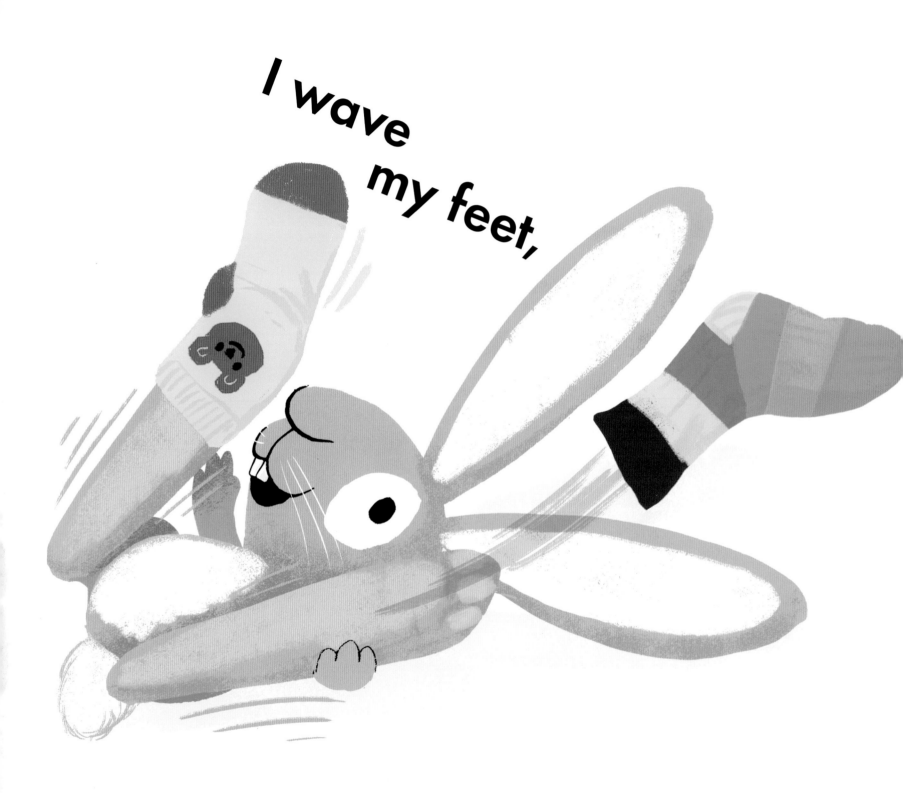

I drum out a beat.

I can't stop wriggling,

I can't stop giggling,

I can't stop popping,

I can't stop hopping.

I spin round about,

I pop
in and **out**.

If I don't stop, I think I'll burst.

But do you know **what?**

I think I'll **stop** first.